AF399478

Abdulaziz Salah
ALDHAHRI

ILLUSION
TRIANGLE

novum pro

© 2024 novum publishing

ISBN 978-3-99146-647-5
Editing: Chris Beale
Cover photo:
Oleksandr Malakov | Dreamstime.com
Cover design, layout & typesetting:
novum publishing

www.novum-publishing.co.uk

Contents

Motivation 7

Search 13

Magic Island 17

Strange world 20

Tribes 26

Black and white 30

Different roots 34

Processing 36

Success 38

Support 42

Sad Day 44

Influential saying 46

Motivation

Cousins Ryan and Bashar, the poorest two young men in the neighbourhood, became rich.

Thus, after they became the heirs of a relative of theirs whom they had not heard of, who lived far from their country.

Fortune has flown on its wings from that far land and landed in the poorest houses in the city.

Although Ryan and Bashar are related, they are also friends and, more than that, they each have a soul that does not rest until seeing the face of the other.

So, as soon as they received the money, they decided together to take a world tour.

They took tourist tours to every beautiful country. They lived in luxury hotels, slept with beauties, tasted all colours and ate at all the world's finest restaurants, drank expensive aged wines and partook in drugs of all kinds.

A few days after returning home from their trip, Ryan woke up from his sleep in the middle of the night, unusually frightened, so he got up from his bed and took turns in the hall talking to himself:

I do not think that the poor are the most miserable creation of God, and the reason is that the poor are always busy searching for things that bring happiness to their heart, and there are so many they are countless.

If he finds something, anything to eat, he will surely be the happiest person, and if luck smiles on him and he watches a movie of any kind or walks around a garden with a cup of coffee or ice cream in his hand, eats a piece of candy, wears shoes, new or even used clothes, etc. Surely, this makes him happy.

The phrase 'etc., etc., etc.' within the list of requirements of the poor is not haphazardly placed. Instead, it carries a message: that the components of the list contributing to the happiness of poor individuals are too numerous to be counted.

How fortunate this poor man is! He may die of hunger, cold, or even disease. Yes, this is possible, but he definitely has hope.

There is always hope. Of course, the poor man lives to the last drop of his life happy, and the reason is that he does not suffer from fear or anxiety.

Dangers and fears surround him. He lives it day and night until it becomes something normal, a part of his life.

So, the poor man dies according to the popular proverb: 'He dies the death of our Lord', unlike the rich.

Yes, the rich 'die the death of our Lord' also, but the difference is that death comes to the poor, while the rich may face death with their wealth and status still intact.

I say this out of experience, not theorising. Just a few days ago, I was on the list of the poor, and now I am on the list of the rich!

The important thing is that sometimes, as I pass through the cemetery, I envy those dead. I feel this feeling sometimes, and 'sometimes' means seven days a week.

While Ryan was walking in the hall, talking to himself, he stopped when he felt pain in his bladder. He rushed to the bathroom, and while he was urinating, he caught a glimpse of his face in the mirror; suddenly he shouted, 'Bermuda Triangle'.

'Yes, the Bermuda Triangle is the solution', and he got out of the bathroom without closing the zipper of his pants while repeating, 'Yes, the Bermuda Triangle is the solution'.

When he came to the middle of the hall, he started talking to himself again:

'The Bermuda Triangle is a marine area located north of the Caribbean islands.

Much has been said about it.

Much has been written about it.

Many movies have been made because of it.

Select the triangle and its shape with imagination.

The strange thing is that its events are old, and we have not heard anything new about it.

Is it fact or myth?

Why did modern civilised man care about it?

Is it because it is mysterious, similar to the mystery of his present and future and occupies his present with it?

Or his nostalgia for the past and its legends?

Alternatively, is the reason emptiness, and he wanted anything, anything, to occupy his mind?

Moreover, he preferred to go on an endless road, perhaps his doing this would end his suffering and keep him busy day and night so that he would not think about things that disturb his peace and awaken him from his sleep.

***

I must take this adventure. I must go to that triangle to find out whether it is fact or fiction.'

Penetrate his ribs, explore his depths, and dismantle his talismans.

Then I will become famous, my name will be repeated in every corner of the globe, and international news agencies will repeat it. Headlines will read:

'Ryan discovered the secret of the mysterious Bermuda Triangle.'

Sure, the story ends so that lovers of mysteries and legends search for a new mystery or another legend as old as history.

It is a dream that I will pursue.

Moreover, while he was thinking about his dream, he heard a knock on the door, so he said in amazement, 'Who is this? Who is knocking on my door at this late hour of the night?'

After hesitating, he hurried and opened the door, and there he was, face to face with his friend Bashar.

He said with joy, 'Bashar, give me good news.'

Bashar said angrily, mocking me: The person who comes late at night has good news.

Ryan: So why did you come so late at night?

Bashar: After this long tour, something strange happened. Boredom leaked into my soul. I am tired of this life, no work, no goal. In fact, sometimes I think about suicide. I think it is the perfect solution to my problem.

Ryan: I am suffering like you. I think, my friend, the best solution is to find a goal or motivation, as Christopher Columbus did. I am sure, my friend, that Christopher was suffering from anxiety and fear as well as frustration.

Bashar: You want to discover a new continent?

If I lived in his time, I would not be disappointed, because everything during his time was available. Opportunities abounded, and life was simple and uncomplicated.

Look around you. There is no more space in this life or a site that has not been drained; history has been read previously and applied and the results have appeared, everything has ended, and you still look at history as a source?

The source, my friend, is over. You live in emptiness. Do you know what emptiness is?

Our life is like a plane whose engines have failed, so our dreams are like this plane that is about to fall.

Ryan: There are definitely undiscovered parts of this world.

Bashar: What do you say?!

The sky is full of satellites. You can watch the world through the Internet. Everything in your world has become clear; your world has become a small village under a high mountain, and you are on this mountain watching everything.

Noting that I did not touch on other unknown devices that were not put on the market.

Ryan: What about, for example, the Bermuda Triangle? Do you know something about it?

Bashar: It is a legend.

It's a myth.

Ryan: What do you say? Ships and planes have disappeared in this triangle, and there is no trace of them to this day.

Bashar: These riddles took place in the sixties.

Have you heard of a similar incident since that time?

They had shortcomings in the field of communication and technology in general, and it was necessary to find a reason to rely on them, and this myth was born.

Ryan: But people and scientists still talk about it.

Bashar: Yes, they speak, so the legend must survive.

Ryan: I don't understand.

Bashar: People do not have the answers to all questions.

What has been resolved or its cause known has become a reality.

What could not be answered remains unknown. This bothers them, so there must be an answer; the myth is the answer to these annoying questions.

Ryan: So, we found the target.

Let's see if the Bermuda Triangle is real or a myth.

Bashar: First, it is a waste of time.

Second, how do we prove that?

Ryan: My friend, you are already thinking of committing suicide because you are suffering from frustration, so what is the importance of time to you?

Then to answer your question as to how?

We have money that we don't need. Let's take a trip to the Caribbean, where the Bermuda Triangle is, and take a cruise to the same areas where planes and ships have disappeared and see what happens.

Bashar: Stop talking. Okay, I give up. I'm ready to go even to hell. What is required of me now?

Ryan: Look, the sun is out, the darkness is gone. There's hope, my friend.

Bashar: Forget the romance now. Tell me what is required of me.

Ryan: What is required is, in fact, that I feel very sleepy, so we have to rest our bodies, even if only for four hours, then we go to the nearest airline agency and buy tickets and travel to the Caribbean. I mean one of the Caribbean countries where the Bermuda Triangle is. This is the first step.

Our next step will be once we get there. What do you think?

Bashar: I agree, Khristov, and I also feel sleepy, but if I go home, I fear that I will lose this opportunity.

Ryan: So let me get you a bed and a blanket. Do you think four hours is enough?

Bashar: Yes, enough, and I don't want you to bring anything. I will sleep on the couch.

Ryan plodded over to his bedroom, looked at the bed for a bit, and then flopped over.

Search

Bashar woke up to Ryan's call, waking him up from his sleep. They headed to the nearest tourism office and booked two seats on a flight to Puerto Rico.

The next day, they boarded a plane that took them to Puerto Rico, passing through another country, and the trip took fourteen hours.

Once they arrived at the hotel, they left their luggage and headed to a restaurant, and from the restaurant to the port, where they found a man in his sixties named Ramos, who had a boat.

They asked him to take them on an open cruise and, although Bashar did not believe in Ryan's crazy idea, he asked Ramos:

'We hear a lot about the Bermuda Triangle. Do you know anything about it?'

Ramos: I know there is an island called Bermuda, that's all I know.

Bashar: But what about the triangle? It is said there is something mysterious, as there are ships and planes that have disappeared.

Ramos: We, like our ancestors, live in the Caribbean, which, as you know, are islands surrounded by a sea, and this sea is characterised by its dangerous coral reefs in addition to its raging storms, and since I am a sailor, I can or am sure that those ships sank as a result of these two factors.

Bashar: You mean that the Bermuda Triangle is an illusion that does not exist?

Ramos: I've been at sea for forty-five years, and I know I could drown just because of those two factors, and I don't believe in this mystical thing, but people love to hear things like this.

Ryan: But you, Ramos, know the sea, but what about the sky? Haven't you heard that there are planes that have disappeared?

Ramos: As I told you, the Caribbean is subject to severe storms. They visit us more than once a year and take away our crops and our homes.

They uproot trees and demolish houses fixed in the ground, let alone moving objects in the sky, and as you notice, these incidents occurred in the sixties and have not been repeated.

I mean for the planes, thanks to satellites, which help to notice these storms and follow their movements.

Ryan could not bear this discussion, so he directed his words to Ramos:

Since you've been at sea for forty-five years, you have enough experience to tell us about the best boats and other mariner's stuff.

Ramos: If you want to help me properly, you should tell me what you want to buy a boat for?

Ryan: There is no secret. We are not looking for treasure. My friend wants to take a trip on the same sea routes that disappeared boats or planes took, to come out of this experience with a satisfactory answer to this mystery. Is it fact or fiction.

Ramos: What's the point of all that?

Ryan: To keep us in this life – give us a motive to live.

Ramos: There are many motives available on these islands, and since you have money, you can achieve them. You are now in the most beautiful spot on Earth. You can buy a farm, as the people of these islands are good people, or you can open a restaurant or an inn. Tourism here is common, and these are real motives. Build a family and live in a beautiful country.

In addition to that, the Americans, with their modern technology, carried out several studies that cost them huge sums of money, and they did not reach any conclusions.

Ryan: Ramos, we came for a specific goal. By saying this, you are wasting your time and ours.

Ramos: Oh, sorry, then there is another solution. I am a man over sixty years of age, and there is not much left, so I am ready to share this crazy journey with you. Sorry, I mean your adventure. You two need a man who knows the sea. I am from this region, and I know the length and breadth of the Caribbean.

Why don't you hire me and pay me in advance because I have financial obligations and it will not cost you much, so what I ask of you will be less than what you need in terms of expenses.

I will ask you for $5,000 dollars a month, and I will take you around the North Caribbean with this boat for as long as you want, and I will be available for you from this moment. In studying the itinerary, what would you say?

Ryan: We both agree.

Ramos: So, the area in which we will do the research is one million square metres, between Puerto Rico, Bermuda, and east Florida.

These are the areas that define the imaginary triangle, which means that we need more than three months for the search process.

Second: Most of the accidents occurred at the beginning of the calendar year, meaning in the winter months, and we are now in November, which means that we will wait for three weeks to begin our journey, and this is what we need to prepare the journey appropriately.

Finally, I want to conclude with the following: I am a man who is older than you; you are the age of my children, and although I am in dire need of resources, what you are doing is a waste of time and money. The Bermuda Triangle is nothing but a legend, and the accidents that occurred, as I told you, are in the winter when there are storms and the sea is agitated. He quickly unfolded the map and said:

And now I want you to see the map. Look, the so-called triangle is located almost in the middle of the globe. Its top is heading to a strait between Florida and Cuba, and its other two sides are reserved for the Caribbean islands from the south, and the other is reserved for the lands of the United States from the northern side, and it represents a spearhead for the waters of the Atlantic flowing into the Caribbean. If you look closely, you will notice that the waters of the Atlantic are confined between four continents from north to south.

This exit is surrounded by islands and reefs connected from the south and a continent from the north, so what happens? The possibility of disaster occurring in this region is possible and it is the work of nature, and now I am finished, so what do you have?

Ryan: Your words are beautiful, Ramos, but we set a specific goal when we left our homes, and we do not intend to back down from it, even if it is flimsy.

Ramos: Then let's sign the contract and hand me $15,000, plus $1,000 for travel supplies.

Magic Island

On the morning of the eighteenth day of December, the three boarded the boat and headed north, leaving the port of San Juan, the capital of Puerto Rico, behind, and continued advancing north until the island and its features disappeared, and everyone saw nothing but the sea on all sides.

Then Ramos stopped the machines, spread the sail, raised his hands, and said: Gentlemen, the wind is our energy, and technology is our confrontation.

Ryan: So, what is your role?

Ramos: I am the man who invented technology and conquered nature.

Bashar: For many years, your human brother will conquer his human brothers, and all these devices will work with remote control, just as children play with devices.

Then there would be no captain or pilot, just closed rooms running everything.

Ramos: And what will happen to the likes of us? How do we live?

Ryan: This question is being asked by a young man, not you.

Ramos did not pay attention to Ryan's provocative answer but continued on his way north, driven by the winds, which were pushing the boat to the east and sometimes to the west.

During that, they would stop at the islands that they passed on their way, and the birds and dolphins would accompany them, as if to support them.

With the first day of the New Year's Eve, they found their way to an island no more than thirty metres long and nine metres wide with a number of coconut trees. Its floor was covered with weeds and beautiful flowers of different colours. It looked like an oasis in the desert.

Ramos said: You will not find, gentlemen, a more beautiful inn than this inn. We will stay in it for a whole day. Despite my long work in the sea, I have never seen an island so small that has such beauty.

They left that island after staying there for a whole day, and the next morning, after they left, fifty-seven miles from that island, Bashar noticed that his head was about to explode, and he felt excruciating pain. When he told Ramos about his pain, he said that he felt the same pain, and so did Ryan.

Then the waves began to collide very quickly, and they noticed that their boat was spinning around itself despite the wind stopping, so Ramos hurried, despite the pain he felt, and lowered the sail and tried to start the engines in an attempt to return to the island from which they had come, and he seemed nervous while trying to start the engines, and he spoke in a strange language to his companions, neither English nor Spanish, as if they were talismans.

All his attempts failed, and the boat started spinning very quickly. Then Ramos asked Ryan and Bashar to tie themselves to the boat and carry knives in their hands to cut the ropes if the need arose, and he returned to his mumblings and vague language. After a few moments, the small crashing waves quickly began to gather together, forming bigger and bigger waves, carrying the boat and moving it between them, and the boat became like a ball that the players moved around, and the waves got bigger little by little as if each one swallowed the other, until they began to diminish and then turned into a very large wave with a mountainous height, and it took the boat high and then descended and carried it again up another to the top.

With these dances, the sound of Ramos' muttering rose as he looked right and left and up and down, and the roaring sound of the sea seemed to rise high, accompanied by rattles and annoying whistling, as a cylindrical column looming connected between the sky and the sea, a kilometre wide, rotating around itself at great speed, heading towards this wave, full of colours. A rainbow, so that the wave carrying the boat rose above its summit as if it wanted to offer it as a sacrifice to this pillar. As soon as this pillar approached, the wave faded away and fell submissively before the pillar to the bottom of the sea. Hence, the boat fell to the bottom and touched the ground, then it rushed at a tremendous speed into this pillar, and for what seemed only a few seconds, Ramos and his companions could see the Caribbean and its islands, and parts of the Americas below them.

For another few seconds, they could see the world inside its blue ball, then, for seconds more, they entered the darkness, and their galaxy, the Milky Way, with its suns and planets, appeared as small points shining in the dark so that this crazy speed calmed down.

Ramos' muttering stopped, and he looked at those around him and said: It's a fact, it's a fact, not an illusion, but, but then what?!

Bashar: Look, look, we are heading to a planet that has a belt. Look at the colours of this belt; it is similar to the colour of the pillar that carries us. How beautiful it is. See, we are approaching it.

Ryan: It might be our last stop.

Ramos: You mean our final resting place.

Everyone noticed that this column was heading towards that planet, which had colours – the colours of the rainbow – while the rest of the planet that was around it was grey.

The boat began to increase its speed, and the contours of the belt began to become clear little by little, so it was a river of water running in the middle of the planet, surrounded by trees, and the boat began to descend like a feather until it descended to the surface of the river.

Strange world

The three noticed that the river was not deep, its width did not exceed half a kilometre, and there were no bends. On both sides there were Caribbean trees and plants. The different thing was the grass filled with colourful flowers, which reminded them of that small island.

The boat began to flow and headed to one of the banks of the river, pushed by the current of the river, which was very slow. Ramos hurried and got off the boat and tied it to a coconut tree, and Ryan looked at him and said: Ramos, you have preceded us to this achievement, you set foot on this land first, and in fact this honour suits you, as your ancestors did it before.

Ramos: But their achievement and their mission reached Mother Earth.

Ryan: What do I hear? If this talk comes from us, it is not surprising, but from you, Ramos?

You are one of the children of those brave explorers.

Ramos: Those discoverers named most of the cities after the cities of the mother country and carried the plants and animals of the mother country with them to the new land.

Ryan: What is the message of this?

Ramos: Their nostalgia for their home country, oh this one, even though they came out poor and frustrated with it, did you get the message?

Bashar: Don't be angry, Ramos. You can call this region New Bermuda. In any case, its climate and vegetation all bear the characteristics of the Caribbean regions.

Add to this that your boat is with you, and it contains some grains from your home country.

Ramos: But my ancestors could connect to the regions they came from. This is the difference, and what a difference!

Ryan: We went back to the same tune, home country, home country.

Ramos: You blame me when I took a step and got out of the boat. See, you two didn't even get out of the boat because of your sense of belonging to it.

Ryan: We wanted the first step to be yours, as you are the oldest of us, in addition to our respect for your ancestors, and we left the first step or honour for you, and here I am filling my hand with the water of this river and drinking it, and from this moment on, priorities will be ours.

As soon as Ryan finished swallowing the water, he shouted: It is delicious, and it is refreshing, so the other two followed him and took a drink. It was only a few minutes after they drank this water everyone felt excruciating pain, severe cramps accompanied by a painful headache, and as a result, they began to writhe in pain, pervading all their bodies, and they did not know which organ they were feeling.

Suddenly, they began to vomit and have diarrhoea; their ears and noses began to bleed, and their eyes began to shed tears continuously.

They stayed in this state for about an hour, and suddenly all those secretions stopped at once, just as they had started.

Each one of them looked at the other. Their bodies were covered with what came out of them so that the colours of their clothes disappeared behind that lava. It looked like it came out of a volcano.

They sat in this state for a while and did not utter a single word, their eyes spinning and their minds wandering.

Finally, Bashar got up and entered the water, and Ramos and Ryan followed him and took a bath.

During that, they felt that their bodies began to get rid of that fatigue and exhaustion, and they all felt very hungry.

So, Ramos went to the boat, took a bag containing some bread, cheese and sweets, and headed to the river bank. Bashar and Ryan followed him while they were shaking, and as soon as Ramos put a piece of bread in his mouth, he started vomiting again. Then Bashar and Ryan pulled their hands from the bag and threw the bread away.

They retreated, trembling from hunger, while they gazed at the sack at times and at others, at Ramos, who was vomiting.

During that, Bashar looked at the hanging bunches of grapes, and, after hesitating, he subconsciously extended his shaking hand, cut a bunch of them, closed his eyes, and devoured them voraciously.

He extended his hand again, cut another cluster and began to devour it without closing his eyes and extended his hand again and again until the shiver stopped and the hunger subsided. Then he cut a number of clusters and threw them towards Ryan and Ramos.

After hesitating, Ryan reached out to the bunches lying on the grass and devoured them with great greed, and Ramos looked at them after the vomiting stopped.

Bashar looked at him and said: Ramos, eat these grapes, they are delicious.

Ramos: Like water, refreshing and delicious?

Bashar, with a broad smile: Try it. If it is delicious and good, it will satisfy your hunger. If it is poison, then what is the point of living alone

Ramos looked at him and extended his hand to one of the bunches of grapes thrown and began to devour it, repeating, 'You have a very convincing style.'

After they devoured the grapes, they waited for the result.

Time passed and nothing happened. Rather, they felt that the blood was running through their veins and that the activity was pervading their bodies, which gave them a sense of reassurance and some of the happiness that they had lost since their arrival on this planet, and they began to exchange conversations and smiles.

Ryan: Can either of you gentlemen explain this strange phenomenon to me?

Bashar: I think that the river water has purified our bodies and rid them of their dirt, and the evidence for that is when Ramos ate a piece of bread that we brought from the Earth, and the body got rid of it, right?!

Moreover, confirming my words, when we ate grapes, nothing happened to us.

Ramos: Your explanation makes sense, and to prove it, drink from the river again.

Bashar: What do you say?

Ramos: I tell you to drink from the river to prove your theory. If what you said is true, nothing will happen to you.

Bashar got up and walked towards the river with slow steps, extended his hand and took a sip of water.

Ramos shouted, saying: One sip is not enough.

Bashar did his part and took more than one sip, then came back and sat under the tree without saying a word, and everyone waited for something to happen. Then Ramos said:

Your theory, Bashar, is correct. He went to the river and drank from it, and so did Ryan, and they did not experience any of the symptoms that occurred to them when they drank from the river water the first time.

Ryan said: Don't you notice that there are no animals, birds, or even butterflies?

There is nothing on this planet other than water, trees, and grass, isn't it strange?

Bashar: I will not explain so that you do not ask me for proof.

Ramos: Yes, it's strange. How did the water and the trees in this strip on this planet come from?

Bashar: You are speaking as if you have wandered into this planet or this tape.

We have not had a time in which you do not see that you are rushing.

Ramos: You are right, Bashar. Now, what is the plan?

Ryan: I think first putting up a sign showing our landing area on this planet.

Everyone got on the boat after Ryan finished writing their three names and made marks on three trees.

Ramos got up, extended the sail and headed right, as the breeze was heading to the right. The boat started moving quietly, heading into the unknown.

And while the breeze of air was pushing the boat straight, everyone noticed the presence of rocks of red, blue, glass, white, and yellow colours of gold on both sides of the river. Then Ramos directed the boat to one of the banks of the river and went down to see these scattered rocks.

As soon as he reached them, he shouted: These stones are treasure, they are rocks of gold, silver and diamonds, they are amazing. So, Ryan called him from the boat, saying:

Ramos, come on board and don't waste our time. You can't benefit from them if they are precious rocks, as you claim.

Where will you sell them, and who will buy them?

Ramos: It's true. I know gold and precious stones very well, but you are right, who will buy them? And he sat on a diamond rock.

In addition, he kept repeating: How much I miss you, Earth.

Bashar: Don't say another sentence, that's enough.

Ryan: Whoa, I found a real thing that you can interact with and look in front of you. Don't you see these metals sticking their heads out of the river?

Ramos: They are American planes. It's Flight 19. Look, there are six planes. There are people, there is company. Don't you notice that the planes are as they were, their colours, their shine, they have not rusted, so let's look for their crews.

Bashar: Its staff? What do you say?

This story happened in 1945 AD. They are dead, and if there are any alive, we will work for them as nurses.

Ramos: Even if that happens, I don't mind. It's nice to have contact with people like you.

Bashar: And what are we? Are we not human?

And for your information, we are younger than you, so you have more time to communicate, but stop mentioning the land and the people of the land.

Ryan: Let us leave that, and let's carry on because there must be other human beings, there must be civilisations here, because that triangle must have sent human beings other than us, and other than those Americans, but the strange thing is that it did not send a bird, goats, deer, or even cows, I'm so craving meat, I have become a vegetarian here.

Bashar: You didn't mention fish.

Ryan: I hate it. Since we got to the Caribbean, ninety percent of the food has been fish and fish products.

Moreover, while they were like this, they fell asleep one after the other, and the boat continued to be pushed forward softly by the breeze.

Tribes

Everyone woke up when their boat shook. They felt that something was pulling them, and they could hear human voices in a strange language. Then they were in front of a group of Inca Indians, and they noticed the presence of huts as far as the eye could see, made of wood and organised in a beautiful geometric shape with a temple in the middle.

These Indians took the three with them and took them to the city, and when they entered, they found children carrying baskets of colourful flowers, and as soon as they entered, the children began to spread these flowers under their feet until they reached a pergola erected near the temple, and seated them.

Other children came carrying baskets with tropical fruits. Everyone was dressed in white, and their shoes were made of wood in a creative way, and they put on their heads hoops made of tree leaves and flowers.

Moreover, a group of men and women came wearing the same dress, but some of its parts were decorated with rainbow colours. They went to a corner in the pergola, in which a sofa was set up, and as soon as they sat down, everyone sat down. Hence, the oldest of them spoke and addressed his words to Ramos, so Ramos was confused because he did not understand a word of what he said and started speaking in English and Spanish. At that point, the old man turned to look at one of the people sitting on the couch. That man stood up and spoke in Spanish, directing his words to Ramos.

Man: The chief asks you: 'When did you arrive?'

Ramos: I really don't know when. We didn't notice the succession of day or night. Since our arrival, we have been in the day, but according to the watch in my hand, we are now.

He looked at his watch, and if it had stopped, he reconsidered and said: I don't know, I don't know, but we haven't had much time.

Man: This means that you have not been here for five days. In this part, we set our times according to the succession of night and day.

The day in this part lasts for five days, and after it comes darkness, to remain for two days. You will get used to this timing, and for those coming from Earth, it depends on a specific date, which is before and after the arrival of the white man.

Ramos: Are there no other human beings in this world of yours?

Man: Yes, there are. There are other races, white and black, and there are a few who live close to us. By the way, there are no women among them, and we do not deal with them and do not allow them to live with or approach us.

Ramos: Because they are single?

Man: No, not for this reason. You are single, and there are no women with you. Despite that, we welcomed you and celebrated with you.

Ramos: So, what is the reason?

Man: Colour is the reason, as you notice that your colour is like our colour, we are all brown, and if we allow these people to enter our world, there will be intermarriage, which will lead to the entry of a new race, and this will threaten us in the future because we have the same colour and the same language, we are one people.

Ramos: Where did you learn Spanish from?

Man: I learned it from the colonisers, as I worked with them.

Ramos: I see you dress differently from the rest and sit on the couch while the others sit on the floor.

Man: We represent the pioneers coming from the Earth, and those sitting on the Earth are our children, grandchildren, and great-grandchildren.

In this part of the universe, there is no death but eternal life.

Ramos: So, you don't have tombs.

Man: Not even doctors, we don't get sick, and we don't die. I mean, any human being who reaches this planet and drinks from this river and washes doesn't get sick or die.

Ramos: Even if he returns to Earth?

The man smiled and said: Are you making fun of me?

But in any case, a person may get sick if he quarrels with someone else, so everyone avoids quarrels.

Ramos: And what kind of disease is this?

The man: Very sad, and if one of them approaches one of us, he feels severe pain, so they prefer to stay away.

Ramos: And when will they recover from this disease?

Man: They never recover from it. It is eternal.

Ryan intervened and said: Ramos, ask him if they have meat, any meat.

Ramos smiled and directed the question to the man:

Man: No, no, my friend, there is no meat in this universe, and as you notice, there is no animal, bird, or even insect.

Ryan: Addressing his words to Ramos, do not translate. I understand.

The interpreter intervened: The leader asks what the news of the Earth is. He got out of it before the white man arrived.

Ramos: The Earth has become a small village in which nationalities have mixed, fused and intermarried. It has developed a lot, and it is difficult to explain what happened during these years, but it is very different according to the difference between your planet and us.

Ramos: When did these pioneers arrive?

Interpreter: As I heard, there is a group who arrived before the appearance of the white man, and others who are few, and I am one of them who left after his appearance. We arrived intermittently, and it was me and my friend, and he pointed to one of the people sitting next to him, the last Incas we arrived here, and then a group of blacks and whites arrived together, and after a time, white men came on board strange bodies.

Ramos: Why didn't you receive them or talk to them?

Translator: No, no, we don't want to be second-class citizens in our land.

What happened on Earth is enough.

We are not bad, but we will not be enslaved again, you understand.

Ramos: In any case, there is no longer slavery, and I think that those in the land now wish that slavery would return so that they could get a job from which they could earn money.

By the way, isn't there another man who speaks Spanish or another language?

Translator: No, there is no one else but me, and I am forbidden to teach anyone. What I did was exceptional and with the prior permission of the leader, as you saw.

Ramos: So, if we want to sit down, how will we communicate with you?

Translator: The leader looks at you as if you are part of the clan; you bear the same colour, and your features are close to us. He believes that we are the children of one man separated by time, and for your information, your communication with us will be easy. Here a person grows until he reaches forty years, after which he stays that age, and I mean people born here. As for those coming from Earth, if their age is under forty years, they grow until they reach this number. For those coming here and their ages are after forty, they keep the age they came with from Earth.

Example: How old are you?

Ramos: I'm sixty-three years old.

Translator: You will stay like this forever, and you have time to learn our language and communicate with us until marriage if you want.

Ramos: What does a man offer to a bride if he wants to marry her?

Interpreter: Nothing. He just chooses the woman he wants to marry and tries to make her laugh. If she laughs, this means that she will accept him, and the tribe will build a hut for them.

Black and white

Shortly after they left the camp, they found three box-shaped huts similar to the huts in the European countryside, and as soon as the boat headed towards them, a group of people dressed as pilots came out.

Ramos and Ryan knew at that moment that they were the American pilots, and as soon as the boat stopped, they found them receiving them, happy with them.

Ramos and Ryan got out of the boat and exchanged greetings, so one of them asked them if they were the new pioneers.

Ryan: Yes, we are the new pioneers, or the new vegans.

Man: First, I introduce you to our leader, Tyler, and I ask him for an excuse to start talking to you without his permission.

Tyler: It's okay, even though the title means nothing to me.

Man: I'm making a calendar, and I'm interested in knowing the date you left the Earth.

Ryan: It was on January 8, 2020 AD.

Man: How many times has the night fallen upon you on this planet?

Ryan: We have not seen the night yet.

The man: Thank you, thank you.

He left them and hurried back to one of the cabins, to the astonishment of Ryan and Ramos.

Tyler: Excuse him, since from the moment we arrived, he kept a note of the number of nights we had to make a calendar.

Ramos: But what about the time that we have spent since the moment we got off the Earth, not to mention the time that you have spent?

Tyler: Please don't discuss this with him. Let him celebrate his achievement. It may be the first and last achievement we will achieve on this boring planet.

Ryan: Boring? It's weird! Lasting health. Eternal life. Look, your clothes aren't worn out.

We saw your plane, and it's in good condition. It's heaven. Although I miss meat. I'm a Caribbean parrot. Bright colours, I eat fruits and nuts and drink just water.

Tyler: So, it's not heaven.

Ramos: I heard you say the boring planet, and I really agree with you, although I have not been on this planet for a long time, and my boredom may be different from yours because I have a family on Earth, and I long for them.

Tyler: I know how you feel. I had a family, too.

Ryan: Didn't you think during this period to find a way to return? You are a pilot and a creative nationality.

Tyler: What's the news on Earth now?

Ramos: I will only talk about your field of aviation, and you can compare it to other things.

Man has reached the moon, and the sky has been filled with satellites that monitor every little thing on Earth, broadcasting television programmes and events at the same time, and there are jet planes that carry more than 400 passengers that reach a speed of more than 600 km/h, and warplanes that exceed the speed of sound, in addition to other planes that fly over the atmosphere, and other things.

This information is issued by a man who works in the sea and has nothing to do with aviation.

Tyler: You say they went to the moon?

Ryan: Yes, but you didn't answer my question.

Tyler: The Earth was created for the sake of man, so its nature provides you with solutions, but here everything is rigid, without obstacles or a goal.

Ramos: Return is a goal, didn't you think to try?

Tyler: It's the same question your friend asked.

We thought of going back during this period to take control of the current coming from the Earth and try to build a plane, but where do we get the materials to build a plane? And if we make it, where do we get the energy needed to operate it? Also, from where do we get strong engines that withstand this current?

He looked at Ryan and said: Our people succeeded because they faced obstacles and thought, and the land helped them find solutions.

Ramos: Your planes are there, and they are in good condition.

Tyler: Where do we get the fuel?

How long does it take us to reach the ground?

How do our engines withstand this current?

Besides, how can we lift planes from the river?

Ryan: Why don't you ask the Incas for help?

Tyler: What do you say? Inca tribes! They wouldn't even let us near them.

Ramos: I spoke to them. They fear you. The white colour represents the coloniser who enslaved them, stole their land and turned their lives into hell.

Tyler: What? Hell? They lived like animals, so the white man came to teach them, treat their patients, rid them of their idolatry, and end their struggles, but you said they hate the white man because he colonised them. There are also blacks who were prevented from approaching them, are they also colonised?

Ramos: They mentioned two reasons, the first of which is that the white man reminds them of the colonised, and the second is that by allowing a white or black man to enter their society, it may allow intermarriage and the emergence of a new colour that creates competition in their society.

Tyler: It's an extreme thought.

Ryan: We read that you are twenty-seven, and I see that you are thirty-one.

Tyler: We are twenty-seven crew members, nineteen Americans, and there are Europeans who arrived before us with a number of slaves.

Ryan: You mean niggers?

Tyler: Yes, niggers.

Ryan: But where are they?

Tyler: They live across the river. You can see their huts from here. He pointed at them.

Ryan: Why didn't you live together?

Tyler: Ha, ha, I don't know.

Ramos: There is a way to lift planes out of the river.

Tyler: What about the other stages?

Ramos: First, we take out the planes. We have thirty-three men in addition to the niggers. We can do the impossible. In this isolation, we need each other. If you agree, I will go to those niggers and ask them for help.

Tyler: In what language?

Ramos: In sign language and love.

Tyler: My men and I are ready.

Different roots

Ramos boarded his boat and went to the site of the Negroes, and they received him and rejoiced in him. By signalling, Ramos discovered that he had a vocabulary that the Negroes understood from him, so some of them understood some Spanish phrases, and Ramos' roots had a great role in understanding with them, as his race was a mixture of Spain and Africa in addition to the race of his Inca ancestors, and this mixture made him close to everyone.

Ramos carried with him in the boat Tyler and Colabali, the leader of the Negroes, and moved while the others followed them along the river, and once they reached the location of the planes, it was dark. It was a pleasant sight for Ramos and Ryan, as this was the first time that this thing had happened for them, so they stopped, contemplating the sky. It was a black board studded with diamonds and precious stones, the colours of the stars around them bore the colours red, blue and green; they were different from the stars on Earth, but they had a flash similar to the flash of diamonds when the light shone on them, and the sky of their planet was decorated with five full moons that had no shortage, which made the general atmosphere romantic and themselves happy.

Tyler approached them, and noticed their distraction and preoccupation, so he joined them and said to them:

Do you see that distant star between the second and third moons? Do you see it?

Ramos: Yes, I see that shining star.

Tyler: Yeah, that shining star, see it, Ryan?

Ryan: Yes, I see it.

Tyler: Do you see a luminous streak of smoke next to it?

Ramos: Yes, I see it.

Tyler: It's our galaxy, the Milky Way.

Ryan: And how did you identify her among the huge number of these stars?

Tyler: It's the pilot's feeling. I love the sky.

Moreover, Tyler continued his speech:

Do you see that thread coming from afar, which is connected to this planet, seeing that it carries the colours of the rainbow?

Ryan said: It is the current that carried us from the ground.

Tyler: Yes, it is, but now, gentlemen, I beg your pardon. I want to sleep because the night is not always available, so it is necessary to enjoy it. By the way, my colleague who asked you about the date of your arrival knew how long the day takes on this planet. It is five Earth days, just as the night is two Earth days, and this is our first achievement on this planet.

Ryan: We heard this from the Incas when we visited them.

Tyler: So please don't tell anyone about it; it might be frustrating for our friend, and now, goodnight. I don't know if this word is appropriate or not.

Ramos: Ryan, this scene needs a fire to be kindled, as it is romantic in this atmosphere.

Ryan: What do you want from fire? You are on this planet. There is no animal, bird or insect, so there is no cooking or grilling.

Ramos: I'm talking about romance, man.

Ryan: You've never been romantic before.

Ramos: I'm living the dream.

Ryan: The Earth is calling you. How many years do you have left to live? It is calling you to tell you.

Ramos angrily: Sleep. We will start work soon.

Processing

Everyone slept, and Ryan spent some time browsing the sky until he fell asleep. After an unknown period of time, everyone got up, one by one, and brought fruits and ate their breakfast.

Tyler asked Ramos what was required.

Ramos: It's still night.

Tyler: What do you want? Do you want us to sleep again?

Ramos: We need four people to cut down the trees to get their trunks, and the rest will bring the fibres of the trees and make ropes from them while I will inspect the plane and take its dimensions.

Tyler: Why the lack of trees?

Ramos: Everything you need is in my boat, and everyone did what was asked of them.

When the first tree fell, one of them shouted: Now I feel like a human, and I belong to the Earth.

The trees continued to be cut. The men dived into the water and put three logs under each wing so that the plane floated, and then Ramos asked Tyler to lower the wheels. They tied the plane from its three legs and pulled it from the river with the ropes that they made from the fibres. They used the same method on the other planes until they took them all out. The last of them was at daybreak and everyone considered it a good omen for them, and they started dancing, and they carried Ramos above their heads as their spiritual leader. Then everyone wondered what the next stage was.

Ramos: The other stages we'll leave to Tyler and his crew.

Tyler: Gentlemen, I participated in this project despite my certainty that its success rate did not exceed one in a million, although practically this percentage cannot happen, but I set this percentage because I know that there are illogical things happening, including our presence here on this planet, and I do not say this to frustrate you, but to encourage you to exert your intellectual and practical energies to make this percentage greater, and to make the impossible a realistic thing, and therefore we need the effort of every individual who stands with us here because this project is our project, so I will explain to you what the problems are that will face us, and you must help us in finding solutions.

The airplanes have been lying in the river for sixty-five years. They need maintenance to operate, and my crew and I will perform this task.

The planes are equipped to carry a specific number, which is six planes, and our number is fifty-two people.

There's enough fuel in the planes to fly for four hours, and we don't know how far it is from here to Earth.

For our travel to Earth, we will fly through the rainbow current that will lead us there. It is a strong current, and we will be flying against it.

In addition to our need for new technology, this we will obtain through Ramos and Ryan, as they are the last to come from Earth, and they may benefit us with some information, especially since they told us that man has reached the moon, and this is an old achievement for them, and there are planes floating above the atmosphere, so we may benefit from them in their description of these planes and any information about them, but for now, gentlemen, I and my crew will take a rest, and then we will try to operate the planes, and I think that you also need to rest and think, and I am ready to hear any suggestion from you.

Success

After Tyler and his crew took a rest, they began to check their planes. The rest supported them by standing with them, encouraging them and helping them when needed. The time for the experiment came, and Tyler and the crew boarded their planes and started operating the engines, and the pleasant surprise was that the engines worked on the first attempt. Tyler moved, followed by the other planes, to the location they chose in advance as their runway. The six planes converged and, at the edge of the runway, they increased the power of the engines, so the first plane rushed quickly and took off, followed by the other planes.

That sound, despite its disturbance, was the most beautiful sound they had heard in their lives, and the view of the planes flying over their heads was the most beautiful sight they had ever seen. The engines stopped so that the remaining crowd rushed to them, congratulating them joyfully, and Tyler and his crew got off the planes.

Tyler spoke with his utmost happiness: Our success rate for the mission is now fifty percent. The planes are ready, so let us now celebrate our achievement.

Ryan: And what do we celebrate with? There is nothing here but fruit. We are here like monkeys. Our real celebration is the day we leave this planet.

Tyler: So quickly find a solution to the fuel problem to go against the current, given that my crew found a solution to make our planes be able to find space to carry additional passengers on them through some modifications.

One of the Europeans said: I have a solution.

Tyler: Speak up, we're all ears.

The European: There is a way to deal with the issue of energy and current together, which is adding propellers to the airplanes that the current will power. The stronger the current, the faster the propeller will catch spin, like the Dutch fans that depend on current in their operation to provide the plane with electrical energy.

Tyler: It's a good idea, but where do we get these fans from? As you can see, we need equipment and ovens, and since I arrived on this planet, I have not seen fire, let alone ovens.

Ramos: The Incas have a solution. I saw them wearing white clothes, and I thought they were silk, but they told me that they were fibres.

Tyler: Where did they get these minerals?

Ryan: Aren't there gold and silver minerals that fill this valley?

Tyler: These metals need smiths. Oh, I mean smiths.

Ramos: The Incas have a solution. I saw baskets they carried made of gold and silver with diamond handles, and these baskets were decorated with precious stones. I also saw on their hands, necks, and legs skilfully made necklaces of gold and precious stones, splendour in accuracy and beauty.

Tyler: We have found a solution for the propellers. Now, the last question I have for Ramos and Ryan, who are able to answer it, is: What is the technology that man has reached in the field of aviation?

Ryan: The most amazing thing that humans have achieved in the field of aviation is the shuttle, which is a plane that is able to fly over the atmosphere and return to the ground propelled by jet engines, and they put a kind of ceramic in the front of the plane to protect it from combustion when it penetrates the atmosphere.

Tyler: It's important information, but where do we get this technology from?

Ryan: We make the noses of planes out of diamonds. It's the hardest mineral on Earth, and it's also available here, so we get home rich, and the Incas will help us.

Tyler: So that's a job for you and Ramos.

Ramos: Can't you make a model of the fan you want out of wood to take to the Incas?

Tyler: Yes, the model will be the engine of the boat.

So, the crew disassembled the engine of the boat and took from it the models they wanted with modifications in the 'feathers' of the propeller and delivered it to Ramos. They asked to make six models for each plane, and Ramos and Ryan carried these models on their boat and headed to the Incas. Upon their arrival, they were greeted by a large gathering of the Incas, headed by their leader. They were captivated by the planes and wanted to know what was happening around them.

Bashar came out of the ranks, pulling a woman by her hand. Once he arrived, he hugged Ryan and Ramos and introduced them to his wife, and then Ramos asked him how did you make her laugh?

He said: I imitated the monkey for her.

After completing the reception ceremony, the leader requested, through his translator, to meet with Ryan and Ramos, so they went to the pergola, and the leader asked Ramos about the reason for his arrival, and what about the UFOs?!

Ramos: These bodies are planes that carry people, and those people and we want to leave this planet. We extracted the planes to bring them back to Earth, but here I am asking you for some favours, so please help me.

Leader: What is this service?

Ramos: In order to arrive, we need additional things such as covering the noses of planes with diamonds, as well as our need to make models of such things (and Ramos showed them to him), and in fact, we do not have knowledge of drafting, and we do not have ovens or even fire, and in short we need you, chief, to help us

Leader: Let those whites return with their tribes and planes and colonise us. No, no, this will not happen.

Then Ramos got down on his knees and began to cry, saying: Chief, I know your suffering and appreciate your concern, but I have a wife, children and grandchildren in the land, and I long to see them. It is the site of sorrows and pains, and since I arrived on this planet, I have not seen a tear for a man, woman, or even a child.

Ramos: If I had my family, I wouldn't wish for another planet, and I wouldn't choose a friend or brother other than you.

Leader: I will not refuse your request, Ramos, even if it threatens our world.

41

***

Support

The leader asked his translator to gather a number of men, take their equipment and leave with Ramos to help him. He went inside the temple, and everyone boarded the boat after carrying the tools they needed. Before they left, Bashar came and boarded the boat with them, and as soon as they arrived, the Inca men headed to a large rock of diamonds, and they began to dig it and make moulds out of it for the models that were given to them from Ramos.

Then, they brought veins of gold and placed them inside these moulds and added grey stones to them, which reacted with the gold at a tremendous speed and turned it into a liquid. It was only a few moments until they took out the first model, while others of the Inca men made diamond chips and stuck them to the front of the planes as requested by Tyler. The work continued until nightfall again, and they worked continuously, resting from time to time, while the crew of Flight 19 installed those golden fans on both sides of the wings. Each wing contained three propellers, and as soon as the day dawned, the six planes appeared as if they were six women standing tall, adorned with diamonds on their necks and gold bracelets in their hands, and everyone looked at them with admiration.

Tyler asked Ramos and the translator to accompany him to the 'City of the Incas', and when they reached the city gate, he asked the translator to meet the leader.

As soon as the leader arrived, Tyler addressed him, saying: Chief, on behalf of everyone, thank you for the help you have provided us, and I accompany this thanks with an apology for what you have suffered. Your ancestors are from the white man, and you should know that the vast majority of our ancestors and those who migrated from their mother country to your homes was a result of their suffering in the country from which they left, and your country was considered a dream for everyone who sought security, and others left for the sake of wealth, and as you know there is a difference between the two demands, and you should know sir, your planet will remain a treasure lost from human eyes, and no one will reach it except those whom nature has sent to you.

Moreover, this is a promise from all my companions and me, and now I ask you to accompany me to see the work we have accomplished and your men had an important role in.

After this reassuring speech, the chief of the tribe rose.

He accompanied them, and when they arrived, the leader shook hands with everyone and wished them a safe return to their homes.

Tyler asked the leader to ride in one of the planes, and he took off and flew over the city of the Incas, and the leader was at the height of his happiness. After a flight that lasted twenty minutes, the leader got off the plane and asked Tyler about their departure time. Tyler told him that he would wait until nightfall to show the rainbow thread, through which they would return to Earth because it could not be seen during the day. Then the leader promised that he would not leave the site until the last plane took off to bid her farewell.

Sad Day

Time passed slowly for the group as they longed for the Earth, the world from which they came.

The time of departure came, and a group of Incas, men and women, led by their children, carried baskets of gold with diamond handles that were filled with fruit. Each member of the departing group was presented with a basket, in addition to flasks made of silver filled with river water, and this made everyone happy, knowing that this water would treat all diseases.

They called it the water of eternal life, and everyone began preparing to board the planes. As night approached, they began to bid farewell to the Incas and their leader.

Bashar went to Ryan and said to him: Ryan, we came out together from the Earth, and I hope that we will stay together.

What do you want to return to?

What do you want on Earth?

Ryan: I don't belong on this planet because I'm not a vegetarian. In addition, I want to go back and celebrate my achievement. Life on this planet is routine and boring.

Bashar: Then go. Everyone has started to climb aboard. Hurry up so that they don't leave you.

Ryan climbed aboard as everyone did, and as soon as it began to get dark, a rainbow thread appeared, so Tyler asked all the pilots to start their engines, and the roar of the planes began to fill the place, and the Inca men, their children, and their women, and with them Bashar, moved away only with their bodies, but not their souls.

Their tear-filled eyes were focused on the fleet of planes, and fear appeared on their faces even though they had not known grief or tears since the first day they arrived on this planet.

The roar of the planes increased, and they moved successively until they reached the runway. Tyler began to take off, and then the squadron followed him, flying behind their leader.

The Inca tribe remained standing with Bashar until those planes disappeared from view, and they withdrew from the site, dragging their feet towards their city.

The five planes began to struggle with that current, which increased as they went deeper into it, and the propellers that the European invented began to rotate strongly whenever the opposite current became stronger, which increased the speed of the planes.

The pilots and those with them saw nothing around them but complete darkness in that tunnel, showing them from one moment to another the lights of stars and objects around them as if they were running their planes at a huge speed over a runway in the sky.

The propellers started spinning faster and stronger until their screeching became unbearable, and the planes began to deviate from time to time. It was no longer possible to find a solution to these deviations despite the pilots trying to keep their planes on one path. Finally, their energies were exhausted, and they surrendered their planes to nature, and they themselves surrendered to sleep despite their attempts to stay awake.

Influential saying

Everyone woke up as the planes began to crash one after the other. Suddenly, the Milky Way appeared, and the spacecraft slowly approached the galaxy and began to shake and deviate more as they approached it until the Earth appeared clearly to everyone as it stood among the other planets revolving around its mother, the sun.

The planes headed towards the ground at an amazing speed, and everyone could see continents surrounded by water and covered by clouds.

The screech of the propellers increased, shared by a loud crackling sound, and strange sounds appeared from inside the plane, such as hissing.

In addition, Ramos looked at the basket that was near him, which was gifted to him by the Inca tribes. Soon it evaporated.

The crackling and deviations increased, and everyone noticed that the propellers, which were made of gold, began to fade, as well as the diamond pieces that were placed on the front of the planes and on their sides.

They noticed that the wings of the planes and the noses began to redden for a few seconds, and then all the planes were rushing with tremendous force back into the current that began to attract them strongly inside and sweep them towards the unknown again, so everyone started screaming and became certain that what they saw was their last covenant on the Earth.

Then Ryan got up from his seat, climbed over the others, went to the door and pushed it with his feet, shouting: No, no, I will not go back, I will not go back.

He threw himself out of the plane into the tunnel and fell, and then he fell from his bed with Bashar on his head.

Bashar: Why did you startle me?

Ryan: Bashar, where is your wife?

Bashar: What is wrong with you?

What happened to you? I don't have a wife!

Ryan: Where am I? Where is Ramos?

Bashar: You are at home, and who is Ramos?

Ryan: In my house? Praise be to God, praise be to God, and he stood up and started looking around, then said to Bashar: Come on, let's go out.

Bashar: Where did you go in your pyjamas? What happened to you?!

Ryan: Oh yeah, and he went to the cupboard and threw off his pyjamas, put on his dress, and said to Bashar: Let's go out.

Bashar: Excuse me, I felt hungry, and I ate some fruit from your fridge. Would you like a banana?

Ryan: What? A banana? Fruit? Take it away, take it away. I'm hungry too. I'm taking you to the fanciest steak house in town.

Bashar: What about the Bermuda Triangle?

Ryan: What is the Bermuda Triangle? I don't want to hear that name.

Do you know, my beloved cousin, that he who said, 'Contentment is an inexhaustible treasure,' was not only a wise man but an experienced man.

Yes, my friend, contentment is a wonderful thing.

Bashar laughed and said: Yes, I remember this sentence well. We used to repeat it when we were poor!

***

On the way to the restaurant, Ryan asked his cousin Bashar, saying:

Are you still contemplating suicide?

Bashar smiled and said: I heard a voice during my sleep repeating: Occupy your soul before it can occupy you.

And he continued his speech: Yes, I will concern myself with reality, not with illusion!

END

The author

Abdulaziz Salah Aldhahri was born in Jeddah, KSA, in 1958. His father worked for the Ministry of Agriculture. Abdulaziz pursued education zealously and, at the age of 17, he joined Saudi Airlines, juggling work with remote university studies, ultimately earning a Bachelor's degree in English Language.

At the age of 46, Abdulaziz retired from the airline and embarked on a new chapter as a writer. He has penned six educational books, ten fictional works, and seven collections of stories.

Beyond his professional accomplishments, Abdulaziz finds immense fulfilment in his role as a devoted family man. Married with six children, he cherishes every moment spent with his loved ones, imparting to them the values of perseverance and integrity.

Today, Abdulaziz stands as a testament to the power of passion and perseverance, his journey from humble beginnings to literary success serving as an inspiration to aspiring writers and individuals alike.